Fancy NANCY

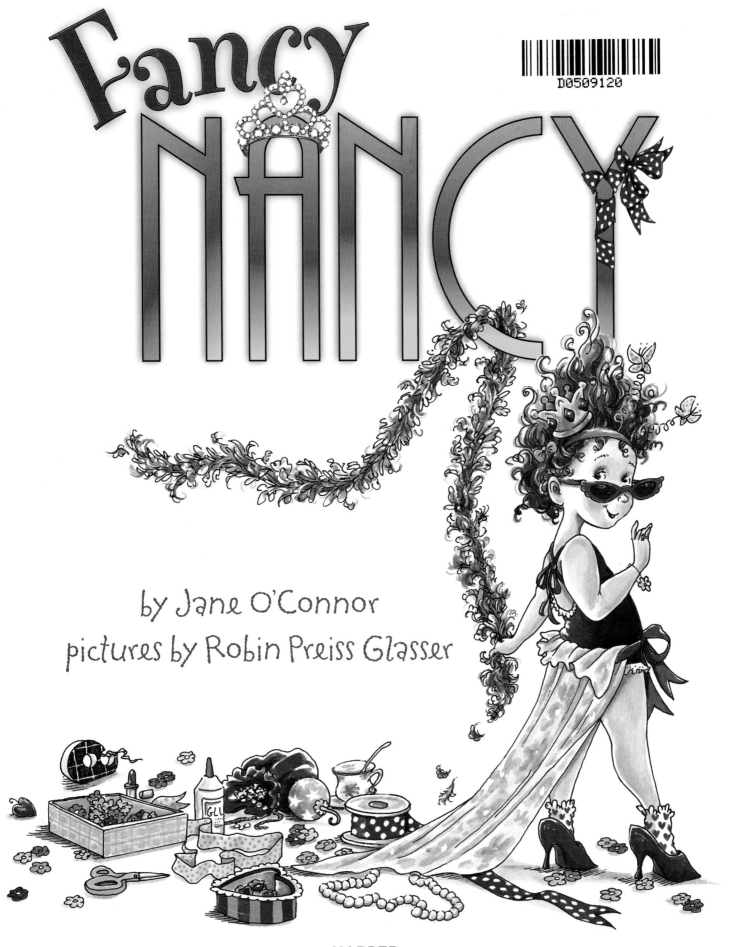

by Jane O'Connor
pictures by Robin Preiss Glasser

HARPER
An Imprint of HarperCollinsPublishers

For Margaret Frith, pal extraordinaire
(that's fancy and French for great)
—J. O'C.

For Jessie, who herself wore
rhinestones to Pre-K
—R.P.G.

This is my room before I made it fancy.

Fancy Nancy
Text copyright © 2006 by Jane O'Connor
Illustrations copyright © 2006 by Robin Preiss Glasser
Manufactured in China.

Library of Congress Cataloging-in-Publication Data
O'Connor, Jane.
  Fancy Nancy / by Jane O'Connor ; pictures by Robin Preiss Glasser.— 1st ed.
    p. cm.
  Summary: A young girl who loves fancy things helps her family to be fancy for one special night.
  ISBN 978-0-06-054209-2 (trade bdg.) — ISBN 978-0-06-054210-8 (lib. bdg.)
  ISBN 978-0-06-184684-7 (intl. ed.)
  [1. Individuality—Fiction. 2. Costume and dress—Fiction. 3. Manners and customs—Fiction. 4. Family life—Fiction.]
  I. Preiss-Glasser, Robin, ill. II. Title.
PZ7.0222Fa 2005   2004028662
[E]—dc22   CIP
                                                                                AC

Typography by Jeanne L. Hogle
10 11 12 13 SCP 10 9 8 7 6 5 4 3
❖
First Edition

I love being fancy.

My favorite color is fuchsia.
That's a fancy way of saying purple.

I like to write my name with a pen that has a plume.
That's a fancy way of saying feather.
And I can't wait to learn French because *everything* in French sounds fancy.

Nobody in my family is fancy at all.
They never even ask for sprinkles.

There's a lot they don't understand. . . .

Lace-trimmed socks *do* help me to play soccer better.

Sandwiches *definitely* taste better when you stick in frilly toothpicks.

A princess is supposed
to keep her tiara on.

"What's a fancy girl to do?"
I ask my doll, Marabelle.
Her full name is Marabelle
Lavinia Chandelier.

Then I get an idea that is stupendous.
That's a fancy word for great.

Maybe I can teach my family how to be fancy.
I make an ad and stick it on the fridge.

Soon there is a knock on my door.
My family saw the ad. They want to get
started right away.

The trouble is, my family doesn't own any fancy clothes.

That's okay. I go find—what is that fancy word?
Oh, yes!—some accessories.

Ooo-la-la! My family is posh!
That's a fancy word for fancy.

My mom twirls in front of the mirror.
"Why don't we go somewhere fancy tonight?"

"How about dinner at The King's Crown?" Dad suggests.
Wow! My parents are acting fancier already.

"May I escort you lovely ladies outside?
The limousine is waiting."

My dad is our chauffeur.
That's a fancy word for driver.

When we arrive at The King's Crown,
everyone looks up.
They probably think we're movie stars.

I am so proud of my whole family.
They eat with their pinkies up and
call each other "darling."

Darling!

"For dessert, *let's* have *parfaits*," my mom says.
"That's French for ice-cream sundaes."

Amazing! My mother knows French!

When our parfaits are ready,
I curtsy and say, "*Merci.*"

I carry the tray like a fancy waiter.

Oops! I trip. I slip.

The tray does
a double flip!

I don't feel fancy anymore.

I want to go home.

After I get all cleaned up, I put on my dressing gown.
Those are fancy words for bathrobe.
I feel much better. I'm ready for a parfait.

I tell my parents, "Thank you for being fancy tonight."

"I love you," my dad says.
"I love you," my mom says.

And all I say back is, "I love you."
Because there isn't a fancy—or better—way of saying that.